NELLA THE PRINCESS KNIGHT: SPARKLE FEST SHOWDOWN!
A CENTUM BOOK 978-1-912564-41-5
Published in Great Britain by Centum Books Ltd
This edition published 2018
1 3 5 7 9 10 8 6 4 2

Centum Books Ltd, 20 Devon Square, Newton Abbot, Devon, TQ12 2HR, UK

books@centumbooksltd.co.uk

CENTUM BOOKS Limited Reg. No. 07641486

A CIP catalogue record for this book is available from the British Library.

Printed in Italy.

SPARKLE FEST SHOWDOWN!

Based on the teleplay by Sarah Jenkins
Adapted by Mickie Matheis
Illustrated by Steph Lew

One sunny day, Princess Nella and her best friend, Sir Garrett, were in Castlehaven's town square, admiring the shiny balloons and glittery banners that decorated the kingdom. The townspeople were celebrating Sparkle Fest.

'It's absolutely, positively my favourite holiday *ever*!' exclaimed Nella.

Every year, one horse from the kingdom was named Sparkle Fest Champion. The winner had the honour of pulling Nella's family to the castle in the royal carriage for the Sparkle Fest Light Show.

'I wonder who the next Sparkle Fest Champion will be!' the princess said excitedly.

'I sure hope it's *meeeee!*' said Nella's best unicorn friend, Trinket. 'Being *sparkle*-tastic is my *thing*!'

'Being Sparkle Fest Champion isn't just about being sparkly – it's also about having fun,' Nella reminded Trinket.

'Totally, Nella,' said Trinket. 'Of course.'

The competition was about to start when
everyone heard a loud crash. Sir Garrett's horse,
Clod, rushing over to enter the contest, had tripped
and fallen into a flower bed.

Nella and Garrett giggled at the silly horse.

'Glad you could make it, Clod,' the princess said
with a smile.

Trinket was surprised to learn that Clod was trying out to be Sparkle Fest Champion. He wasn't sparkly at all!

'Being Sparkle Fest Champion is *my* thing,' said Trinket. '*I'm* the sparkly one.'

The first event was the Prance-Off, where the horses danced their way across the stage. Tossing her shiny mane, Trinket dazzled the crowd with her perfect rhythm.

Clod came next, and his dancing left the crowd speechless. His hooves moved wildly in every direction. But he looked like he was having a great time.

Trinket was pronounced the winner of the Prance-Off, and Clod congratulated her enthusiastically. 'Good job, Trinket!' he said. 'That was so fun! The Speed Race is next. Race you to the track!'

When Clod sped away, he immediately stepped into a flowerpot. He didn't even notice that it was stuck to his hoof.
Nella and Garrett giggled as the horses lined up to race.

Nella raised her hand. 'On your marks, get set, GO!'
Clod was so busy talking about how much he loved running, he didn't realize the other horses had sprinted away.

During the race, Clod was far behind the others. Then he noticed an ice cream cart at the end of the track. He made a mad dash for it – leaving the other horses in a cloud of dust!

'Clod is our winner!' Nella announced to the cheering crowd.

Trinket was stunned. Whoever won the third and final event would be named Sparkle Fest Champion.

Clod trotted over to her. 'Hey, Trinket, I just wanted to say I'm having so much fun with you today.'

But Trinket wasn't having fun. How could she have fun if she didn't win?

The last event was a jumping contest. Trinket and Clod put on an awesome show! Clod wowed the crowd with his rock-star moves while Trinket enchanted them with her fancy dance poses.

She did her best. But would it be enough? She'd have to wait and see what the judges decided.

Nella held up her hands to quiet the crowd. 'This year's Sparkle Fest Champion is... TRINKET!' she said.

Trinket twirled around with delight.

'... AND CLOD!' Nella continued. 'It's a tie!'

Clod was thrilled, but Trinket couldn't believe her ears. Being Sparkle Fest Champion was her *thing*! She didn't want to share it with Clod.

When it was almost time for the light show, Nella hitched Trinket and Clod to the royal carriage. A pretty ribbon connected their harnesses.

'Okay, your harnesses are attached, and you're ready to go. Have fun!' Nella told them. King Dad, Queen Mom and Princess Norma climbed into the carriage.

Clod was so happy to be next to Trinket.

'Look at us!' he said. 'One little ribbon holding together two Sparkle Fest buddies! Gosh, without that ribbon, you'd be pulling this carriage all alone.'

'Really?' Trinket said. That gave her an idea. 'Clod, look over there – a kitten!'

When Clod looked away, Trinket pulled the flimsy ribbon loose and quickly trotted off with the carriage.

Watching from the grandstand, Nella called, 'Trinket! You're leaving Clod behind!'

Trinket looked back to see Clod's sad face. Even though she really wanted to be the only Sparkle Fest Champion, she couldn't leave her friend.

But when she tried to stop the carriage, the harness snapped!

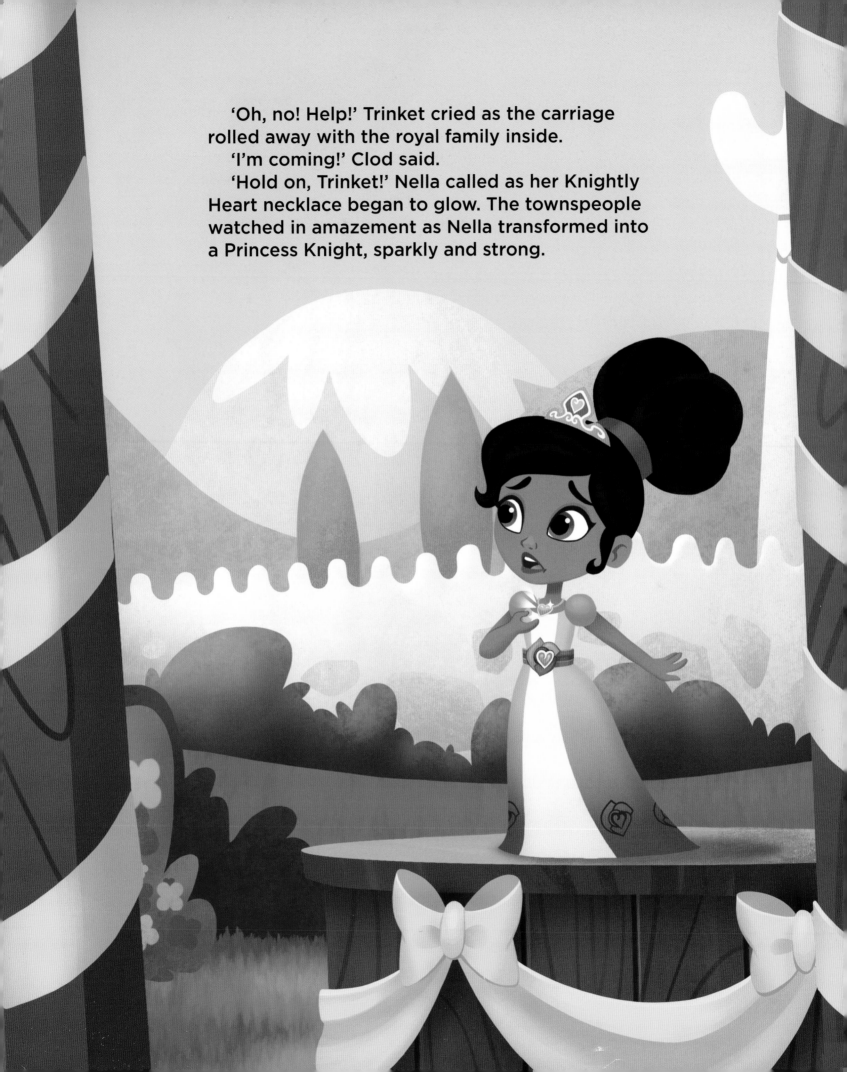

'Oh, no! Help!' Trinket cried as the carriage rolled away with the royal family inside.

'I'm coming!' Clod said.

'Hold on, Trinket!' Nella called as her Knightly Heart necklace began to glow. The townspeople watched in amazement as Nella transformed into a Princess Knight, sparkly and strong.

Nella had to act fast to save her parents and baby sister! She tossed her sword into the air, and it turned into a bow with a brightly coloured ribbon.

She grabbed an arrow and shot it into a tree branch, then used the ribbon to swing down from the grandstand.

Nella landed on her feet on the backs of Trinket and Clod. She gripped their reins and charged after the runaway carriage.

'Thank goodness you're here!' Trinket said, relieved. 'I'm so sorry! I made a big mistake!'

'It's okay, Trinket,' Nella said. 'Right now we have to work together to fix this. Follow that carriage!'

Just as they were gaining on the carriage,
it hit a rock, which made it turn sharply and
hurtle down a steep hillside! Nella, Trinket
and Clod charged after the carriage.

'Hold on, Mom and Dad!' Nella called.
'We're coming!'

Trinket and Clod finally caught up with the carriage. Nella quickly reattached their harnesses to it just in time. They were heading straight towards a ravine!

Nella thought quickly. 'We have to jump over the ravine!'

'We'll never make it!' Trinket protested.

'Yes, we will,' Nella replied. 'It's like the Jumping Contest – you guys were great at that. But you have to work together as a team. Get ready – on the count of three. One... two... THREE!'

With that, Trinket and Clod leapt over the ravine. The horses and the carriage landed safely on the other side.

'Way to go!' Nella cheered.
'We did it!' Clod said.
'And doing it together was actually... *fun*!' Trinket added.

With the royal family safe, Nella and her
friends hurried to the castle for the light show.
'Would you like to do the honours?' Nella
asked Trinket and Clod.
Smiling happily, the pair flipped the switch
together, lighting up the castle in a brilliant
display of colour.
It was the best, brightest Sparkle Fest ever!

READING TIPS

★ We hope you and your child enjoy reading this picture book.

★ Try to make time to read with your child every day and make reading together something you both look forward to.

★ A good way to bring a book to life is to put on different voices for different characters in the story.

★ You could also stop at certain points in the book to ask your child what they think about the characters, what is happening in the story and what they think might happen next.

★ You can still read aloud to your child, even when they are confident enough to read by themselves.

★ If your child is excited by what they are reading, it will help them to retain their interest in reading.

★ A love of reading can last a lifetime!

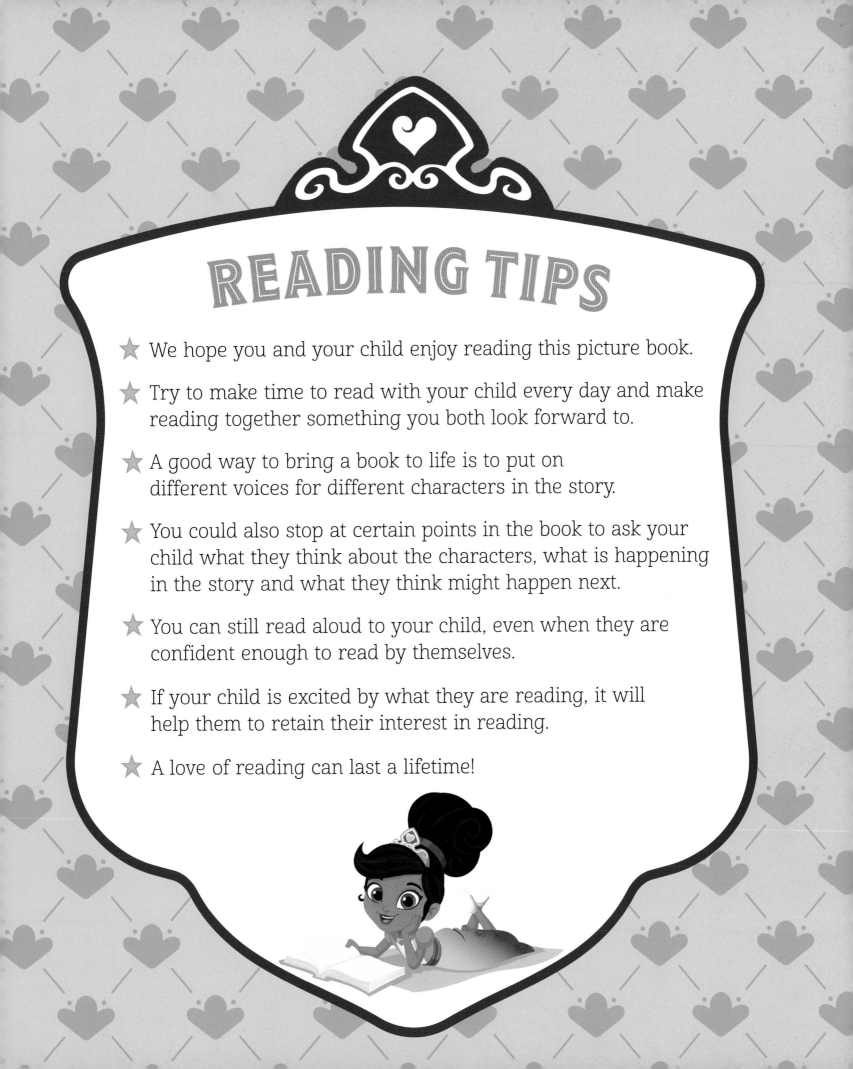